OKLAHOMA

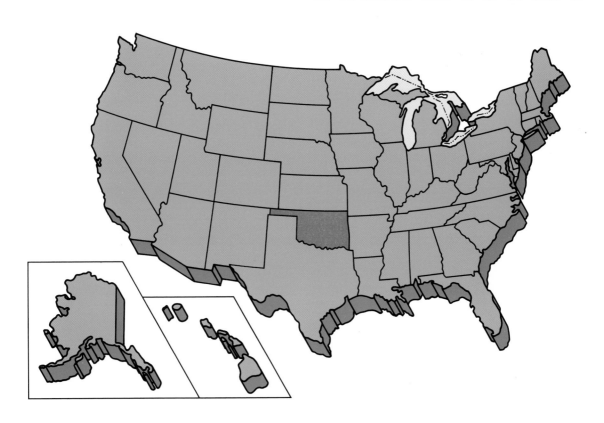

OKLAHOMA

Rita C. LaDoux

Lerner Publications Company

This book is available in two editions:
Library binding by Lerner Publications Company
Soft cover by First Avenue Editions, 1997.
241 First Avenue North
Minneapolis, MN 55401
ISBN: 0-8225-2717-0 (lib. bdg.)
ISBN: 0-8225-9783-7 (pbk.)

LIBRARY OF CONGRESS
CATALOGING-IN-PUBLICATION DATA
LaDoux, Rita.
    Oklahoma / Rita C. LaDoux.
      p.   cm. — (Hello USA)
    Includes index.
    Summary: Introduces the geography, history,
people, industries, and other highlights of Oklahoma.
    ISBN 0-8225-2717-0 (lib. bdg.)
    1. Oklahoma—Juvenile literature.
[1. Oklahoma.] I. Title. II. Series.
F694.3.L34 1992
976.6—dc20   91-14444

Manufactured in the United States of America
2 3 4 5 6 7 8 9 10 - JR - 05 04 03 02 01 00 99 98 97

Cover photograph courtesy
of Oklahoma Tourism/Fred
W. Marvel.

The glossary that begins on
page 68 gives definitions of
words shown in **bold type** in
the text.

 This book is printed
on acid-free, recycla-
ble paper.

CONTENTS

Did You Know . . . ?

☐ Per square mile, more tornadoes strike Oklahoma than any other state. One hundred and one twisters touched down in Oklahoma in 1982.

☐ Two elephants ran away from a circus near Hugo, Oklahoma, in 1975. The elephants were able to hide in the area's thick woods for two weeks before they were found.

❑ Oklahoma is a leading peanut-growing state—only five other states produce more. A concrete peanut, claimed to be the world's largest peanut by the town of Durant, honors some of the state's peanut farmers.

❑ The Dual Parking Meter Company set up the country's first parking meters in Oklahoma City on July 16, 1935. The charge for parking was a nickel.

❑ Oklahoma is the only state in which wells have been set up to pump oil from the grounds of the state capitol.

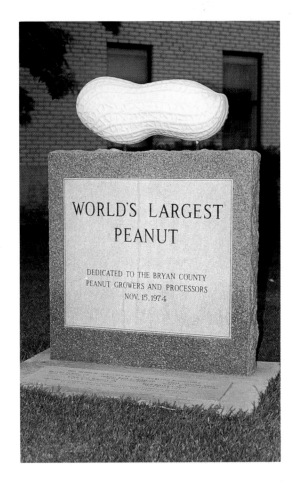

WORLD'S LARGEST
PEANUT

DEDICATED TO THE BRYAN COUNTY
PEANUT GROWERS AND PROCESSORS
NOV. 15, 1974

A Trip Around the State

Oklahoma takes its name from two Choctaw Indian words, *okla* (people) and *homma* (red). Oklahoma lies in the south central United States. Four states—Texas, New Mexico, Colorado, and Kansas—surround the Oklahoma Panhandle, a long, narrow strip of land that extends west from northwestern Oklahoma. Texas (to the south) and Kansas (to the north) continue all the way to Oklahoma's eastern border. There, Oklahoma meets Missouri and Arkansas.

A stream flows through northeastern Oklahoma *(above).* In western Oklahoma rise the Wichita Mountains *(opposite page).*

9

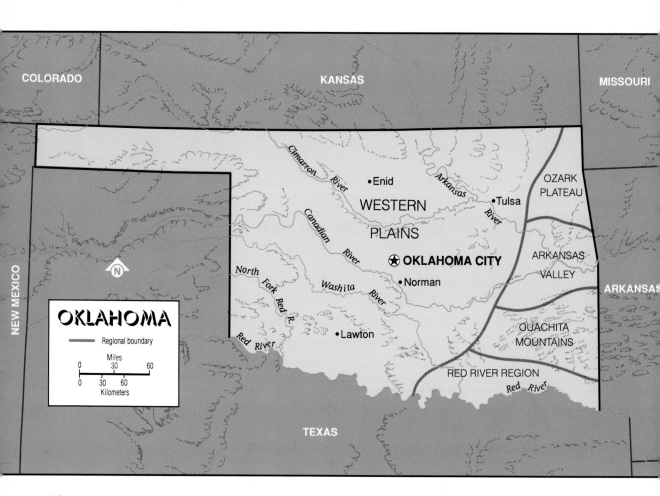

COLORADO
KANSAS
MISSOURI
NEW MEXICO
ARKANSAS
TEXAS

Cimarron River
•Enid
Arkansas River
•Tulsa
OZARK PLATEAU

WESTERN PLAINS
Canadian River
⭐ OKLAHOMA CITY
ARKANSAS VALLEY

North Fork Red R.
Washita River
•Norman

Red River
•Lawton
OUACHITA MOUNTAINS

RED RIVER REGION
Red River

OKLAHOMA
Regional boundary

Miles
0   30   60
0   30   60
Kilometers

10

Oklahoma has many different landforms. But the state can be divided into five geographic regions. They are the Ozark Plateau, the Arkansas Valley, the Ouachita Mountains, the Red River Region, and the Western Plains.

The hills of the Ozark Plateau roll into northeastern Oklahoma from Missouri and Arkansas. Millions of years ago, underground pressures pushed this region above the land around it, creating a high **plateau**. Rushing rivers have cut deep valleys into the plateau.

The Arkansas Valley, a region covered by grassy plains and forested hills, is south and west of the Ozark Plateau. The Arkansas River runs east through the valley toward Arkansas.

A river winds through the tree-covered hills of the Ouachita Mountains.

South of the Arkansas Valley lies the Ouachita Mountains, the most rugged region in the state. Spring-fed rivers carve through the region's low valleys, and forests blanket the mountains' high ridges.

11

The Red River winds slowly past the Red River Region. At one time, the river regularly flooded the surrounding plains after heavy rains. Although floods still occur, dams now keep the river from overflowing as often as it used to. Peanuts and cotton are raised in the Red River Region.

The Western Plains stretch across the western two-thirds of Oklahoma, from the Red River Region to the end of the Panhandle. Mountains jut up from the southern part of the Western Plains, but low hills blanket most of the region. In the Panhandle, **mesas** (flat-topped hills) dot broad **prairies,** or grasslands. The Panhandle is also part of the Great Plains, a huge region that extends from Texas to Canada.

Wide, grassy prairies *(above)* and rugged hills cover the Western Plains. These hills *(right)* are called the Glass Mountains because their peaks are covered with sparkling layers of the mineral gypsum.

13

Two large rivers, the Red and the Arkansas, flow through Oklahoma. The Red River forms Oklahoma's southern border with Texas. Rivers in southern Oklahoma, including the Washita and the North Fork, pour into the Red River. The Canadian, Cimarron, and several other rivers feed the Arkansas River, which runs through northeastern Oklahoma.

Although Oklahoma has some natural lakes, people created the large lakes in the state when they built dams to block the flow of rivers. The water released through some of these dams spins engines that create **hydroelectric power**. This power fuels lights and machines in homes and businesses.

Swimmers play in the pool below Turner Falls, a waterfall in the Western Plains.

A tornado strikes the Oklahoma prairie.

In the skies over Oklahoma, cold air flowing south from Canada runs into warm, moist air flowing north from the Gulf of Mexico. This makes Oklahoma's weather very quick to change. Strong winds often blow across the state, and violent tornadoes sometimes twist through the area in the spring and summer.

Snow blankets a park in Oklahoma City.

Temperatures and rainfall can change a lot from day to day, but most of Oklahoma is usually warm and dry. Summer temperatures average 82°F (28°C), but they sometimes climb as high as 120°F (49°C). Winter temperatures generally stay above freezing. The Panhandle gets only about 15 inches (38 centimeters) of rain and snow each year, but the muggy Red River Region can get more than 50 inches (130 centimeters) a year.

Short prairie grasses grow on most of the dry western half of Oklahoma. This was once grazing

Armadillo

Prairie dog

land for huge herds of buffalo, and is still home to smaller animals—coyotes, armadillos, rabbits, and prairie dogs.

Tall prairie grasses once waved over the plains of eastern Oklahoma. Much of this land is now planted with crops. In the eastern hills, pine, pecan, walnut, sweet gum, and oak trees grow. These forests provide homes and food for deer, opossums, raccoon, mink, and foxes.

Oklahoma's Story

The earliest people in what is now Oklahoma came to the area more than 10,000 years ago. These Native Americans, or Indians, lived on the plains and hunted buffalo and mastodons—huge animals that looked like hairy elephants.

By A.D. 600, another group of Indians had moved into the region. These Indians are called mound builders because they built large earthen mounds, or hills. The Indians buried their dead in some of these mounds and worshiped the sun and the four seasons on top of other mounds.

The mound builders planted fields of corn, squash, and tobacco in the fertile Arkansas Valley. No one knows what happened to these people. Dry weather in the 1300s may have caused their crops to fail. If so, they probably starved to death or moved away in search of food.

Europeans knew little about the land where the mound builders once lived. Some believed Indians lived in cities of gold. In 1541 Spanish explorer Francisco Vásquez de Coronado searched North America for these golden cities.

The mound builders constructed a town near present-day Spiro, Oklahoma, where their burial and temple mounds still stand.

Francisco Vásquez de Coronado found groups of Wichita Indians living in grass houses like this one, which was built in the 1800s.

Instead of gold, Coronado found groups of Indians who lived in small villages, hunted buffalo, and grew corn. Although Coronado discovered no riches for himself, he and other explorers left a treasure for the Indians—horses. With horses Indians could leave their fields to ride after the millions of buffalo on the Great Plains.

Soon the Cheyenne, Comanche, Kiowa, Osage, Pawnee, Wichita, and other Indian tribes were hunting buffalo in what is now Oklahoma. These tribes spoke many different languages and had different customs, but all the tribes hunted buffalo and lived on the Great Plains. They became known as the Plains Indians.

20

Plains Indians sometimes disguised themselves in wolf skins *(upper left)* to get closer to a buffalo herd. Once the Indians had horses, though, they could hunt buffalo by riding after them *(lower left)*. After a hunt, the Plains Indians carved the buffalo bones into tools, made the skins into clothes and tepees, and cooked the meat over fires fueled by buffalo chips.

The Plains Indians did not know it, but in 1682 France claimed their hunting grounds. France made them part of Louisiana, a vast piece of land in North America. In 1803 France sold Louisiana to the United States in a deal called the Louisiana Purchase.

At the same time, many Europeans were sailing to the United States. As the country grew more crowded, its citizens wanted more land. Some wanted land in the southeastern United States that belonged to five different Indian tribes—the Choctaw, Chickasaw, Cherokee, Creek, and Seminole.

To make more room for the new settlers, the U.S. government pushed these Indians west. In the 1830s, the five tribes were forced to move to a part of Louisiana called the Indian Territory. This territory covered parts of what are now Oklahoma, Kansas, and Nebraska.

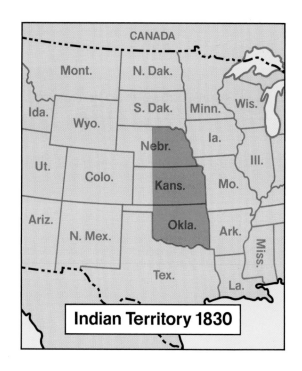

Indian Territory 1830

The Trail of Tears

The trip from the southeastern United States to Oklahoma was long and hard for the Choctaw, Chickasaw, Cherokee, Creek, and Seminole tribes. Some groups of Indians were taken to Oklahoma in old, unsafe steamboats or wagons. Other groups were forced to walk thousands of miles to their new homes. The tribes were often moved in the winter, but they were not given shoes, warm clothing, or enough food. Many people suffered from frostbite. Others starved, froze, or died of disease. So many Indians died during the Cherokee removal of 1838 *(above)* that the journey is called the Trail of Tears.

23

The five tribes—the Choctaw, Chickasaw, Cherokee, Creek, and Seminole—lived very differently than the Plains Indians did. For example, the five tribes built many of their buildings, including the Choctaw council house *(left),* like the buildings of European settlers.

The land that is now Oklahoma was divided among the five tribes. Each of the tribes governed its own nation and made its own laws. The tribes built towns and farms and opened schools.

Just as they had in their former homes, some Indians built **planta-tions** (large farms) and used black slaves to work in the fields. The use of slaves throughout the southern United States was causing many arguments. Northern lawmakers wanted to outlaw slavery. But Southerners wanted slaves to work on their plantations. These differences led to the Civil War, or the war between the North and the South, which broke out in 1861.

In 1865 the North won the Civil War. The Union (North) punished everyone in the Indian Territory whether they had fought for the South or not. The territory was reduced to the area that is now Oklahoma. The government squeezed the five tribes into the eastern half of this territory. Then the government moved some of the Plains Indians, as well as tribes from all over the country, to **reservations** (land reserved for Indian tribes) in the western part of the Indian Territory.

Indians were often not allowed to leave their reservations to hunt. Many tribes depended on the U.S. government for food. Here, the Cheyenne Indians wait for their flour, sugar, and meat.

Cowboys drove their cattle across Oklahoma to Kansas, where the animals were shipped to markets in the east.

long-horned cattle from Texas across Oklahoma.

Next came the railroads. In the 1870s, workers laid track across Oklahoma for the Missouri-Kansas-Texas Railroad. Shopkeepers set up stores along the tracks, and towns grew up around the stores.

With the cowboys, railroads, and towns came the end of the Indians' way of life. Many cowboys drove cattle across Indian land without asking permission. Cattlemen rented vast pieces of land from the Indians for some of Oklahoma's first cattle ranches.

As more tribes moved into the Indian Territory, so did white people. Between 1866 and 1885, cowboys drove more than six million

Railroad builders sent hunters out to shoot herds of buffalo because the animals destroyed tracks and slowed trains.

White hunters also destroyed one of the Indians' sources of food by shooting huge numbers of buffalo. The hunters skinned the animals and left their bodies to rot on the Great Plains. By 1885 millions of buffalo had been killed, and only about 200 were left.

Another threat to the Indians came from the east. By the 1880s, settlers had spread throughout much of the United States. Most farmland across the country had been claimed. People thought the Indian Territory was the last place left to get their own land. Settlers called Boomers hurried to the territory, hoping to "boom" onto Indian land.

The U.S. Army forced the Boomers to leave the territory, which still belonged to Indian tribes. But

Settlers who snuck onto the Indian Territory before the Land Run of 1889 and illegally claimed the best land were called Sooners, because they came too soon. Here, soldiers throw Sooners out of the territory.

Settlers race for land in the town of Guthrie.

Boomer leaders convinced the government to buy a small piece of land, called the Unassigned Lands, from the Indians. Settlers would be allowed to move onto this land on April 22, 1889.

At noon on April 22 the Land Run began. More than 50,000 settlers raced in wagons, on horses, or on foot to claim plots of land. By the end of the day, the cities of Guthrie and Oklahoma City had sprung up and grown to more than 8,000 people each.

Among the settlers who claimed land in the Land Run were many black families *(left)*. Just over one month after the Land Run, Guthrie's main street *(below)* was lined with new buildings.

So many settlers moved to the Indian Territory in 1889 that the U.S. government divided it in half. The eastern half was still the Indian Territory, owned by Indian tribes. The western half, including the Unassigned Lands, became the Oklahoma Territory.

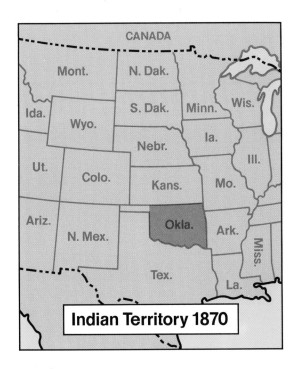

Indian Territory 1870

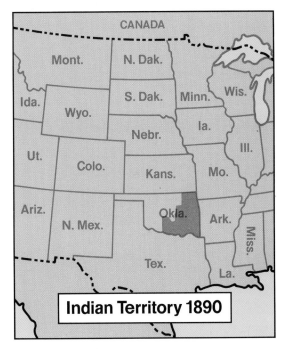

Indian Territory 1890

In the early 1900s, so much oil lay beneath the ground in Oklahoma that some wells gushed for days before workers could stop them.

The Oklahoma Territory's new settlers soon wanted more of the Indians' land. The government took each tribe's land and divided it into separate plots, called allotments. Each tribe member got a small plot. But the government made more plots than there were tribe members. Then the government bought the leftover land and gave it to new settlers who poured into the Oklahoma Territory.

Not all of the newcomers wanted farmland. Some of them wanted to mine the oil that had been discovered beneath Oklahoma's soil. Oil was needed to fuel homes and factories. Mining grew, along with ranching and farming, as railroads carried Oklahoma's products to markets on the country's East Coast. Railroads also brought more **immigrants** (newcomers) to the territory from the eastern United States and from Europe.

As the Oklahoma Territory's population of new settlers grew, many people wanted the region to become a state. People living in the Indian Territory wanted their territory to be a separate state called Sequoyah. But the U.S. government decided to admit both territories as one state. On November 16, 1907, the two territories became Oklahoma, the 46th state. In this new state, fewer than one out of every five people was an American Indian.

Settlers kept coming to Oklahoma. Many of them hoped to strike it rich in the oil business. During the early 1920s, more oil was pumped in Oklahoma than in any other state. Workers drilled thousands of wells. Many of the wells spewed so much oil, known as "black gold," that their owners made a fortune.

When oil was discovered on Osage land, the tribe became rich. During the oil boom of the 1920s, some tribe members became millionaires.

In 1921, a group of whites in Tulsa threatened to kill a black man, who had been accused of attacking a white girl. When some African Americans gathered to protect him, a riot began. In the fighting, white rioters destroyed more than $1 million worth of buildings in the black community, and at least 80 people were killed. Within a year, black Tulsans had rebuilt most of their homes and businesses.

But in the 1930s, the Great Depression hit the United States, leaving people short of money. Oil and beef prices dropped. Many businesses closed. Farmers had to sell their crops for very low prices.

During the Dust Bowl of the 1930s, a farmer and his children run from the dust storm that has begun to bury their shack *(left)*. In Hooker, **Oklahoma** *(opposite page),* a dust cloud billows over the streets.

By 1933 there were few crops left to sell. A severe **drought,** or dry spell, hit the Great Plains, drying the land and killing thousands of acres of crops. Farmers had cleared their fields of trees and plowed up prairie sod, leaving no roots to hold the state's soil in place. Oklahoma's strong winds whipped the dry, dusty soil into people's homes, food, and water. Clouds of dust five miles (eight kilometers) high blocked out the sun. Part of Oklahoma became known as the Dust Bowl.

Thousands of Oklahomans left their dried-up farms and headed to California, where they hoped to find jobs. When the drought finally ended in 1939, Oklahoma's farms were in bad shape. But people had started planting trees to block the wind, and farmers began growing crops with roots strong enough to hold down the soil.

Oklahoma's flag has an Osage Indian shield with seven eagle feathers. Two symbols of peace—a peace pipe and an olive branch—cross in front of the shield.

By 1941 many farms had recovered. That same year, the United States entered World War II (1939–1945). The military needed wheat, beef, and oil. Farmers, ranchers, and oil drillers now had plenty of work. Oklahomans built airfields and military bases in their state, where the flat land was ideal for training pilots and soldiers.

During World War II, many Oklahomans moved to cities, where people took jobs in factories to make supplies for the war. By the war's end in 1945, more people lived in cities than on farms. The state's larger cities, such as Oklahoma City and Tulsa, had grown up near oil and natural gas fields. Many businesses across the country needed these fuels to run machinery. As other states bought more oil and gas from Oklahoma, it thrived.

Since World War II, Oklahoma has built many new businesses. Oklahomans can earn a living not only from oil and farm products but also from other goods, such as plastics and mobile homes. Now, when oil prices drop, some Oklahomans can turn to other businesses for money.

After the war, refineries were built in Oklahoma to clean the state's oil before it was sold to factories.

10,000 B.C. A.D.600 1541 1682

Early Indians hunt mastodons in what is now Oklahoma

Mound builders settle near present-day Spiro

Francisco Vásquez de Coronado searches for golden cities

The king of France claims Louisiana

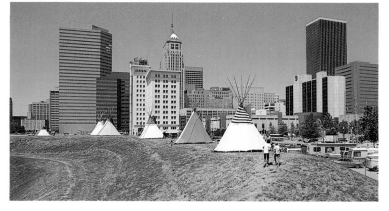

Tepees stand in Oklahoma City during the Red Earth Native American Cultural Festival.

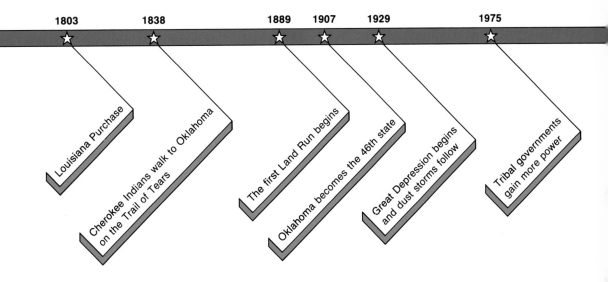

1803 — Louisiana Purchase

1838 — Cherokee Indians walk to Oklahoma on the Trail of Tears

1889 — The first Land Run begins

1907 — Oklahoma becomes the 46th state

1929 — Great Depression begins and dust storms follow

1975 — Tribal governments gain more power

Oklahomans of all different backgrounds are also learning to accept each other. Native Americans have won more power to govern their tribes, and Indian groups are working to regain some of their native land. Some day all Oklahomans may share their state's riches.

Living and Working in Oklahoma

More American Indians live in Oklahoma than in almost any other state. Members of more than 60 tribes make up 6 percent of the state's population, or about 220,000 people. Many Indians live in cities and towns. Others live on tribal lands.

Some of Oklahoma's Native Americans live in **Tulsa** *(opposite page).* A Creek man, a member of one of the 67 Indian tribes in Oklahoma, dresses in traditional clothing for a powwow *(right).*

Children dance at the Czech Festival in Yukon, Oklahoma.

Nearly 86 percent of all Oklahomans have European ancestors. Seven percent of Oklahomans are African American. Others are Hispanic or Asian.

Most of Oklahoma's 3.1 million people live in **urban** areas (cities) in the eastern part of the state. Oklahoma's two largest cities are Tulsa, a center for the production of oil and airplanes, and Oklahoma City, the state capital. Lawton, Norman, and Broken Arrow are the next largest cities.

Compared to some other states, Oklahoma doesn't have many big urban areas, and much of the state is still **rural** (countryside). In the Panhandle, miles of prairie separate farms and towns.

Cherokee Indians at the Tsa-La-Gi Ancient Village make spears as their ancestors did, carving the weapons from stone and wood.

Indian culture is important to many Oklahomans. At Tsa-La-Gi Ancient Village near Tahlequah, Cherokee Indians demonstrate how their people built villages and farmed before Europeans came to North America. At Anadarko, the Southern Plains Indian Museum displays arts and crafts of the Plains Indians. Dancers and drummers gather in Anadarko each August for the American Indian Exposition, one of the largest pow-wows in the United States.

A statue at the National Cowboy Hall of Fame honors Buffalo Bill.

At the Gilcrease Museum in Tulsa and at the National Cowboy Hall of Fame in Oklahoma City, visitors can view both Western and Indian art. History buffs can tour the town of Guthrie, which looks much like it did when Oklahoma was a new state. And at a museum in Claremore, comedian Will Rogers is remembered for his funny sayings and writings.

Oklahoma sports fans have plenty of games to choose from. Professional teams in the state include the Tulsa Zone and the Oklahoma City Cavalry basketball teams. For many football fans, the game between Oklahoma State University and the University of Oklahoma is the sports highlight of the year.

46

The state is known for horses—rodeo horses, show horses, and racehorses. Professional riders rope cattle and ride broncos at rodeos all over Oklahoma. Horses race at Remington Park in Oklahoma City and parade at the World Championship Quarter Horse Show.

A rider clings to his horse during a rodeo in Guymon, Oklahoma.

48

People in Oklahoma can go fishing, horseback riding, or zooming over sand dunes *(opposite page)*. Some Oklahomans can even be found at pie-eating contests *(right)*.

Oklahomans enjoy swimming, waterskiing, fishing, and boating on the state's many lakes. Deer, ducks, and wild turkeys attract hunters each fall. Dune-buggy drivers race at Little Sahara State Park. And hikers and campers explore hills and caves in the state's parks and forests.

Soldiers at Fort Sill fire a practice round.

Just as Oklahomans enjoy many different kinds of recreation, they also work at many different jobs. The largest number of Oklahoma's workers have service jobs, or jobs helping other people or businesses. Teachers, salespeople, and doctors perform service jobs. Oklahomans who work at military bases, such as Fort Sill and Tinker Air Force Base, also have service jobs.

After services, manufacturing earns most of the state's money. Mechanics build the machinery used to pump and refine (separate and clean) oil and natural gas. Other workers refine the oil and gas. At some factories, Oklahomans use refined oil to make tires and plastic products. Still other Oklahomans build engines and airplanes at plants in Tulsa.

Four percent of the state's workers are miners, but they earn 10 percent of the state's money. Oklahomans pump oil and gas from the state's 100,000 oil wells and 25,000 natural gas wells. Workers then pipe the oil and gas to other states, where the fuels supply energy for cars, homes, and factories. Oklahoma's miners also dig for coal and gypsum, a whitish mineral used in plaster and candy.

Workers finish an airplane wing at a plant in Tulsa.

Cattle graze on the wide prairie.

The state's ranchers graze their cattle on Oklahoma's grasslands and then fatten the cows in feed lots before selling them to meat-packing plants. Wheat, the state's largest crop, grows on the northern and southwestern plains. Oklahoma farmers also raise pigs, chickens, cotton, peanuts, soybeans, pecans, and watermelons. Five percent of the state's workers farm and ranch.

Although Oklahoma has many industries, the oil and gas industry affects more Oklahomans than most others. When fuel prices are low, many workers lose their jobs

Hot-air balloons rise into Oklahoma's sky.

and have little money to spend. But when oil and gas sell for high prices, more jobs open in the oil industry. People in this field earn high wages. When these workers have more money to spend, many Oklahomans—from salespeople to doctors—benefit.

Pumps pull oil from wells in Oklahoma.

Protecting the Environment

In ancient times, seas and swamps covered much of Oklahoma. As the tiny plants and animals that lived in these areas died, they sank to the bottom and were slowly covered by rocks and soil. Over millions of years, the pressure of these layers of rock and earth turned the dead plants and animals into natural resources called **fossil fuels.**

The passing centuries have left three kinds of fossil fuels in Oklahoma—oil, natural gas, and coal. Oklahomans mine and sell these fuels. People in Oklahoma and other states also use these energy sources to power their cars and heat their homes. Fossil fuels employ thousands of Oklahoma's workers and bring millions of dollars into the state. But Oklahoma's fossil fuels are limited.

Some natural resources can be renewed, or replaced. To make sure future generations don't run out of wood, for example, people can plant trees. But fossil fuels cannot be renewed. Once the fuels have been mined, they cannot be replaced. Over the last 100 years, miners have dug up much of what took millions of years to create.

A natural-gas miner adjusts the valves on a gas well.

Geologists look for more oil and gas on the plains of central Oklahoma, where most of the state's fossil fuels have been found.

To find more fossil fuels in Oklahoma, **geologists,** or people who study the earth, inspect the state's land surface and underground rock for the familiar signs of oil, gas, or coal. The geologists then try to predict where more deposits of fuels will be found.

57

At oil companies, lab workers search for new ways to mine fossil fuels.

Scientists have also developed ways to get more oil out of mines that were thought to be empty. For example, some miners shoot water or steam deep into these wells. The steam thins the oil and flushes it out of cracks in the well. Miners can also remove oil from shale, a type of rock that gives off oil when it is heated.

To avoid using up Oklahoma's fossil fuels, many Oklahomans are trying to use less fuel rather than finding more deposits of fuel. A few ways to save fuel are to drive cars that use less gas and to carpool. Oklahomans can save some of the energy needed to run air conditioners and furnaces by keeping their homes warmer in the summer and cooler in the winter.

Recycling also saves fossil fuels. Some people help collect and recycle plastic containers such as milk jugs, which are made from oil. Car oil can be cleaned and reused.

Oklahomans bring their used car oil and antifreeze to a recycling drive in Tulsa.

Dams use waterpower, not fossil fuels, to create energy. The force of the water flowing through the dam turns engines that make electricity.

Another way to make sure Oklahoma does not run out of fossil fuels is to use other forms of energy. Other sources of power—even human legs and feet—can replace fossil fuels. Instead of driving cars, some Oklahomans walk or ride bicycles. Waterpower, instead of coal or oil, is used to make electricity in some parts of Oklahoma. Scientists are also looking for ways to use the power of the wind and sun to meet energy needs.

Oklahomans want to use their natural resources wisely. Conserving, or using less, and recycling will make the state's fossil fuels last longer. But Oklahomans are also concerned about making a living. As people use less fuel to conserve for the future, Oklahomans might have to find new sources of money.

By working together, miners and conservers may also be able to save both jobs and fossil fuels for future Oklahomans.

Oklahomans both young and old work to guard the resources of their state.

Oklahoma's Famous People

CATTLE ANNIE
(left)
LITTLE BREECHES
(right)

ADVENTURERS

The Bill Doolin Gang was famous in the 1890s for its many successful bank and train robberies. The gang's members included the young outlaws Cattle Annie and Little Breeches. One of the gang's favorite hideouts was in Ingalls, Oklahoma.

Wiley Post (1899–1935) was the first pilot to fly around the world alone in an airplane. Post, born in Texas, grew up in Oklahoma. He and his friend Will Rogers were killed when Post's plane crashed in Alaska.

Thomas Stafford (born 1930), an astronaut, has flown on three space missions, including one trip to the moon. Stafford was born in Weatherford, Oklahoma.

THOMAS STAFFORD ▶

▲ WILEY POST

MICKEY MANTLE ▶

ATHLETES

Mickey Mantle (1931–1995) hit 536 home runs during his baseball career with the New York Yankees. Born in Spavinaw, Oklahoma, Mantle was named Most Valuable Player in the American League three times and was elected to the Baseball Hall of Fame in 1974.

62

Jim Thorpe (1886–1953), a Sauk and Fox Indian born near Prague, Oklahoma, was sometimes called the best all-around athlete in the world. Thorpe won Olympic gold medals in track and field, was an outfielder for three baseball teams, and played professional football for 15 years.

◀ JIM THORPE

BUSINESS & RELIGIOUS LEADERS

Oral Roberts (born 1918), a preacher and missionary, was born near Ada, Oklahoma. Roberts preaches his religious beliefs on the radio, on television, and at meetings all over the world. He founded the Oral Roberts University in Tulsa.

Sam Walton (1918–1992) was the founder of Wal-Mart, a chain of stores known for their low prices. Born in Kingfisher, Oklahoma, Walton was one of the richest people in the United States.

SAM WALTON ▶

BILL MOYERS ▶

JOURNALISTS

Paul Harvey (born 1918), from Tulsa, Oklahoma, is a broadcast journalist for ABC News. His daily radio program, "Paul Harvey's News and Comment," is heard all over the country. Harvey also writes a newspaper column for the *Los Angeles Times*.

Bill Moyers (born 1934), a journalist from Hugo, Oklahoma, began his career as an assistant to President Lyndon B. Johnson. Moyers has worked for the PBS and CBS television networks and has won 18 Emmy Awards for his television shows.

63

LaDonna Harris (born 1931) is the founder and president of Americans for Indian Opportunity, an organization that works to make tribal governments stronger. Harris, who is part Comanche Indian, is from Lawton, Oklahoma.

Jeane Jordan Kirkpatrick (born 1926), from Duncan, Oklahoma, was the first woman to serve as the U.S. ambassador to the United Nations. Kirkpatrick teaches political science and has written several books about the U.S. government.

Wilma Mankiller (born 1945) was the principal chief of the Cherokee Nation, the second largest tribe in the United States, from 1985 to 1995. She is the first woman to hold that office. Born in Stilwell, Oklahoma, Mankiller inherited her last name from a warrior ancestor.

◀ LaDONNA HARRIS

▲ WILMA MANKILLER

JEANE KIRKPATRICK ▶

▲ WOODY GUTHRIE

MUSICIANS & DANCERS

Louis W. Ballard (born 1931) is a composer who uses Native American themes in his music. He has written three ballets and many pieces of music for orchestras. Ballard, a Quapaw–Cherokee Indian, was born on a reservation in Miami, Oklahoma.

Woody Guthrie (1912–1967) was a singer and composer born in Okemah, Oklahoma. Guthrie wrote more than 1,000 children's songs and folk songs, including "This Land Is Your Land."

Maria Tallchief (born 1925) and Marjorie Tallchief (born 1927) were born in Fairfax, Oklahoma. Maria was the first lead ballerina of the New York City Ballet and founded the Chicago City Ballet in 1981. Marjorie was the solo ballerina for the Paris Opera Ballet Company for five years. The Tallchief sisters are part Osage.

MARIA TALLCHIEF *(far right)*
MARJORIE TALLCHIEF *(right)* ▶

◀ RALPH ELLISON

▲ WILL
ROGERS

N. SCOTT
MOMADAY ▶

WRITERS

Angie Debo (1890–1988), a writer and historian, came to Oklahoma Territory in a covered wagon in 1899. She became an expert on Oklahoma history and wrote several books, including *Oklahoma: Foot-Loose and Fancy-Free.*

Ralph Waldo Ellison (1914–1994) grew up in Oklahoma City. A teacher and writer, he was best known for his novel *Invisible Man,* which won the National Book Award in 1953.

N. Scott Momaday (born 1934) is a writer and teacher from Lawton, Oklahoma. The son of Kiowa Indians, Momaday won the Pulitzer Prize in 1969 for his book *House Made of Dawn.*

Will Rogers (1879–1935), born in Oologah, Oklahoma, wrote several books and a weekly newspaper column. He was also a world-famous actor, rope-trick artist, and comedian. Rogers, who was part Cherokee Indian, died in a plane crash in Alaska.

65

Facts-at-a-Glance

Nickname: Sooner State
Song: "Oklahoma!"
Motto: *Labor Omnia Vincit*
  (Labor Conquers All Things)
Flower: mistletoe
Tree: redbud
Bird: scissor-tailed flycatcher

Population: 3,145,585*
Rank in population, nationwide: 28th
Area: 69,903 sq mi (181,049 sq km)
Rank in area, nationwide: 20th
Date and ranking of statehood:
  November 16, 1907, the 46th state
Capital: Oklahoma City
Major cities (and populations*):
  Oklahoma City (444,719), Tulsa (367,302),
  Lawton (80,561), Norman (80,071),
  Broken Arrow (58,043)
U.S. senators: 2
U.S. representatives: 6
Electoral votes: 8

*1990 census

66

Places to visit: Will Rogers Memorial in Claremore, Grand Lake o' the Cherokees in northeastern Oklahoma, Spiro Mounds Archaeological State Park in Spiro, Indian City U.S.A. in Anadarko, Gilcrease Museum in Tulsa

Annual events: International Finals Rodeo in Oklahoma City (Jan.), World Championship Cow Chip Throwing Contest in Beaver (April), Pawnee Bill Wild West Show in Pawnee (May), Red Earth Native American Cultural Festival in Oklahoma City (June)

Natural resources: oil, natural gas, fertile soil, coal, granite, copper

Agricultural products: beef, winter wheat, hay, corn, cotton, peanuts, chickens, hogs, peaches, pecans

Manufactured goods: oil-field machinery, pumps, boilers, tires, refined oil, aircraft and aircraft parts

ENDANGERED SPECIES

Mammals—Ozark big-eared bat, Indiana bat, gray bat

Birds—American peregrine falcon, black-capped vireo, whooping crane, bald eagle, red-cockaded woodpecker, interior least tern

Fish and Shellfish—longnose darter, Neosho madtom, Ouachita rock pocketbook

WHERE OKLAHOMANS WORK
Services—55 percent
   (services includes jobs in trade; community, social, & personal services; finance, insurance, & real estate; transportation, communication, & utilities)
Government—20 percent
Manufacturing—13 percent
Agriculture—6 percent
Mining—3 percent
Construction—3 percent

CONST 3%
MIN 3%
AGR 6%
MFG 13%
GOVT 20%
SERVICES 55%

Cheyenne (shy-AN)

Chickasaw (CHIHK-uh-saw)

Choctaw (CHAHK-taw)

Comanche (kuh-MAN-chee)

Coronado, Francisco Vásquez de (kawr-uh-NAHD-oh, frahn-SIHS-koh BAHS-kayz day)

Kiowa (KY-uh-waw)

Osage (oh-SAYJ)

Ouachita (WAHSH-uh-taw)

Seminole (SEHM-uh-nohl)

Tahlequah (TAL-uh-kwaw)

Tsa-La-Gi (JAH-lah-gee)

Wichita (WIHCH-uh-taw)

Glossary

drought   A long period of extreme dryness due to lack of rain or snow.

fossil fuel   A material such as coal or oil that is formed in the earth from the remains of ancient plants and animals. Fossil fuels are used to produce power.

geologist   A scientist who studies rocks to learn about the history of the earth.

hydroelectric power   The electricity produced by using waterpower. Also called hydropower.

immigrant   A person who moves into a foreign country and settles there.

mesa An isolated hill with steep sides and a flat top.

plantation A large estate, usually in a warm climate, on which crops are grown by workers who live on the estate. In the past, plantation owners often used slave labor.

plateau A large, relatively flat area that stands above the surrounding land.

prairie A large area of level or gently rolling grassy land with few trees.

reservation Public land set aside by the government to be used by Native Americans.

rural Having to do with the countryside or farming.

urban Having to do with cities and large towns.

Index ▬▬▬▬▬▬▬▬▬▬▬▬▬▬▬▬▬▬▬▬▬

70

Acknowledgements:

Maryland Cartographics, pp. 2, 10; Harvey Payne, pp. 2–3, 8, 12–13, 13, 57; Jack Lindstrom, p. 6; Shauna Plyler/Durant Chamber of Commerce, p. 7; Al Myatt, Area Forester, Oklahoma Department of Agriculture/Forestry Services, pp. 9, 52; Oklahoma Tourism/Fred W. Marvel, pp. 11, 14, 16, 19, 41, 42, 44, 45, 47, 48 (all), 49, 50, 53, 61, 69, 71; © 1992 NOAA/Weatherstock, p. 15; Outdoor Oklahoma, the official publication of the Oklahoma Department of Wildlife Conservation, p. 17 (left and right); Annette Hume, Oklahoma Historical Society, p. 20 (#14998); Independent Picture Service, pp. 21 (top), 64 (center); Library of Congress, pp. 21 (bottom), 27, 36; The Philbrook Museum of Art, Tulsa, Oklahoma, p. 23; Western History Collections, University of Oklahoma Library, pp. 24, 28, 30 (top), 39; Jos. Hitchens, Oklahoma Historical Society, p. 25 (#16575); Oklahoma Historical Society, pp. 26 (#8687), 32 (#19389), 35 (#15583.B); Oklahoma Territorial Museum, Oklahoma Historical Society, pp. 29, 30 (bottom); George W. Parsons, Mitscher Collection, Oklahoma Historical Society, p. 34 (#3191.5); G. L. R., Oklahoma Historical Society, p. 37 (#16575); Mike King, p. 43; Scott Berner/Visuals Unlimited, p. 46; McDonnell Douglas, p. 51; William J. Weber/Visuals Unlimited, p. 54; Apache Corp., American Petroleum Institute, p. 56; Phillips Petroleum Co., American Petroleum Institute, p. 58; Oklahoma State Department of Health, p. 59; Everett Krute, Sand Springs, OK, p. 60; Division of Manuscripts, University of Oklahoma Library, p. 62 (top left); Lockheed, p. 62 (top right); NASA, p. 62 (center); Stew Thornley, p. 62 (bottom); Pro Football Hall of Fame, p. 63 (top); Wal-Mart Stores, Inc., p. 63 (center); Chase Roe/Retna Ltd., p. 63 (bottom); Americans for Indian Opportunity, p. 64 (top left); Cherokee Nation of Oklahoma, p. 64 (top right); Woody Guthrie Publications, Inc., p. 64 (bottom); Chicago City Ballet, p. 65 (top right); The Library and Museum of the Performing Arts, Dance Collection, p. 65 (top left); Station KSTP, Minneapolis, p. 65 (center left); Bern Schwartz, p. 65 (center right); Linda Fry Poverman, p. 65 (bottom); Jean Matheny, p. 66